THE NUTCRACKER

Soon it will be Christmas. The tree has arrived, and brings the scent of forests into my room. I unpack the box of decorations: coloured candles, bright globes and a fairy which will be placed at the very top. She is old now, like me. She is made of a sugared plum which has long ago grown hard and discoloured, and the dress is faded. I turn her over in my hand, and the strains of music come to me, waltzes and polkas, rich and sweet in my memory. I see people dancing, hear the swish of their gowns and the patter of their feet on the polished floor. At the bottom of the box is a toy wrapped in tissue paper, and I unfold it carefully and look at the chipped painted face of a wooden nutcracker. Now I remember the best Christmas I ever had, when I was still a child, and magic things could happen.

For Lily
I.B.

For Alice and Ellen Helliwell
B.D.

THE NUTCRACKER
A DOUBLEDAY BOOK 0385 604378

Published in Great Britain by Doubleday,
an imprint of Random House Children's Books

This edition published 2002

1 3 5 7 9 10 8 6 4 2

Text copyright © Berlie Doherty 2002
Illustrations copyright © Ian Beck 2002

Designed by Ian Butterworth

RANDOM HOUSE CHILDREN'S BOOKS
61-63 Uxbridge Rd, London W5 5SA
A division of The Random House Group Ltd.

RANDOM HOUSE AUSTRALIA (PTY) LTD
20 Alfred Street, Milsons Point, Sydney,
New South Wales 2061, Australia

RANDOM HOUSE NEW ZEALAND LTD
18 Poland Road, Glenfield, Auckland 10, New Zealand

RANDOM HOUSE (PTY) LTD
Endulini, 5A Jubilee Road, Parktown 2193, South Africa

THE RANDOM HOUSE GROUP Limited Reg. No. 954009
www.kidsatrandomhouse.co.uk

A CIP catalogue record for this book is available from the British Library.

Printed and bound in Singapore

THE NUTCRACKER

Written by
Berlie Doherty

Illustrated by
Ian Beck

DOUBLEDAY

It was Christmas Eve. The entire household was bustling with preparations for a party: crackling log fires were lit in the grand rooms, wreaths of bright-berried holly were hung from the doors, and the tree, the great shivering tree of the forest, was carried into the main hall. Franz and I helped to decorate it with candles and baubles and sweets, and then my father lifted me high on his shoulders to place the sugared plum on the top branch. Mama had dressed it to look like a fairy in a spiky red dress, and it smiled down at us as if it could really see us.

My father's important government friends had been invited to the party, and all our relatives were to come too, our young cousins and our own friends, and best of all, our godfather Drosselmeyer. My brother and I longed for him to come, because he was so mysterious and so clever, because he could perform magic conjuring tricks, and most of all, because he had promised us wonderful presents.

How the day dragged. I took out all the dolls that my father had brought me from his travels to the lands of coffee and chocolate, tea and spices. I dressed them up in their exotic costumes, red taffeta and green embroidered silk, golden flowing robes and shimmering cloaks.

"Look, Franz, aren't they beautiful?"

But my brother wasn't interested in my dolls. He lined up his toy soldiers, blackened their boots and polished up the buttons on their scarlet jackets. We played under the tree in the big drawing room, and the lights from all the candles glowed on the coloured sweets spiralling from the frosted branches. The members of the orchestra arrived and began tuning their instruments in the great hall where the dancing would take place. The fire was lit in there, the candelabra flickered diamond lights. My stomach fluttered with the butterflies of anticipation. I kept gazing at the clock, but his hands crept so slowly round his white face that I wondered whether he had stopped completely.

"Soon," Mama promised. "They'll be here soon. Tidy your toys away now. Listen! Here they come!"

I pressed my face to the cold glass of the window. Now I could hear the jingle of bridles and the swish of wheels; I could see snowflakes swarming like white bees in the light of carriage lamps. Our guests were arriving! They came skating and slipping and sliding, clinging to each other and laughing, holding up swaying lanterns, their capes swirling around them; and they brought the sharp night and the snow in with them. They rubbed their hands in front of the great fire, their voices bubbling with excitement. Franz ran to kiss our cousins and grandparents and to be told how grown up he looked in his velvet suit. But I stayed hidden behind the long curtain, my face pressed to the window, looking out anxiously. And there, yes, there was Godfather Drosselmeyer. At last! Now the party could really start!

The orchestra struck up as he strode in with snow still sparkling in his hair and his beard. His black cloak billowed out as he swung round to greet us all, revealing a scarlet lining with pockets bulging with presents. He clapped his hands and we ran to him, leaping round him as he joked and teased: no, he didn't have any presents – yes he did, he had a Harlequin puppet for my cousin Anna, and he made it dance as if it were alive, dance and spin and drop to the ground in sleep. No, he didn't have any more presents – yes he did, a Columbine puppet for Anna's sister. No, no more. Ah yes, for my brother Franz, a golden ball. No, that was all. Why, had he forgotten someone?

"Clara," he said to me, "why do you look so sad?"

And at last he gave a flourish that made us all clap and cheer. "Something very special for Clara," he said, "for a little girl who is growing up."

He looked at me gravely and then he gave me my present. My nutcracker.

How I loved my nutcracker. It was made in the shape of a wooden man with a smiling painted face and arms and legs that moved smartly up and down. I ran to show him to my parents and my grandparents, and Franz ran behind me, shouting that surely the nutcracker had been meant for him. It was a soldier all in scarlet and black like the ones in his toy box.

"But he's not a soldier," I said. "He's a prince."

"He's a soldier prince," Godfather Drosselmeyer told me, and he bent down and whispered, with great mystery in his voice, "Take care of him. Don't let any mice get at him, will you now?"

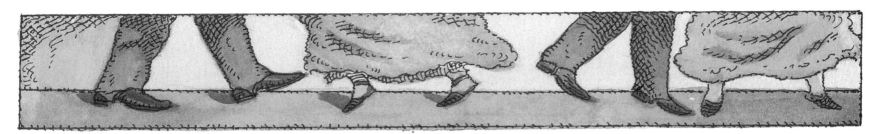

"Mice?" How strange my godfather was! I promised I would always look after my nutcracker, but my brother wouldn't leave me alone. He wanted it for himself. I ran away from him among the swaying dancers and he dodged after me, trying to snatch it out of my hands. We both clung on, each pulling one of the painted legs, and then a terrible thing happened. My nutcracker snapped in half. I was heartbroken. Franz ran away and hid, but Godfather Drosselmeyer folded his long bony hands over the two halves and chanted some quiet magic words, and mended my nutcracker for me.

"Now don't touch him for a bit!" he warned me. "Hide him in the big sofa till later."

And I did, and I'm sorry to say that for the rest of the party I forgot all about him. Franz and I ran off to join in the dancing, and then to eat and drink the party food, and then I was carried up to bed because I was too tired to climb the stairs. But I couldn't sleep. I lay in bed listening to the distant strains of music and the chatter and laughter of the grown-ups. The party ended, goodbyes were called. I heard the guests leaving and the snap of their boots on the icy paths outside, the swish of carriage wheels, and the house sank into silence. The old clock struck midnight, and I sat up with a sudden start. My nutcracker!

I slipped out of bed and picked up my candle. The house creaked and whispered as I crept down the stairs, and all the shadows slid out of the cupboards to frighten me. The drawing room was ghostly white with the light of the frosty moon. I tiptoed to the big sofa and there he was, just as I had left him, hidden under the embroidered cushion. I curled up next to him. Now at last I could go to sleep.

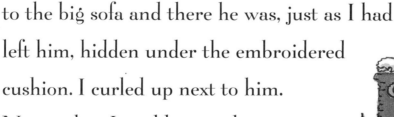

But just as I was drifting away I heard a scrabbling and squeaking, and I opened my eyes to see an army of mice tumbling into the room, growing as they ran till they were as big as dogs, and led by their fierce grey king. I was too frightened to move, but I clung tightly to my nutcacker. "Go away!" I sobbed. "You can't have him."

Then I heard a clicking of heels and a muffled drumming and piping. The lid of my brother's toy box was pushed open and out marched his toy soldiers. They advanced on the mice, growing taller with every step, and their brave swords flashing in the firelight. The Mouse King swung round to glare at me. He snapped his sharp teeth, his tail flicking this way and that like a whip.

"My enemy!" a voice said, and I realized it was my nutcracker speaking. He struggled out of my hands, stretching out his arms and legs, and leapt down from the sofa to stand at the head of the soldiers. He and the king of the mice circled each other. Cannons boomed, the air stank of the smell of powder and smoke, soldiers roared and screamed.

There was such a skirmish of brown and red bodies, and such a mist of smoke that I couldn't see what was happening any more.

"Don't kill my nutcracker," I shouted, and I rushed to stand at his side, hurling my slipper with all my strength at the Mouse King. He fell at our feet, and my nutcracker pierced him with his sword. Instantly the fighting stopped. The army of mice squealed in terror and scurried to their hiding places, hauling their dead king behind them. And I saw that my nutcracker was no longer a little soldier but a prince, taller than me. He held out his hands to me.

"You saved my life," he said. "Long ago the Mouse Sorcerer turned me into a nutcracker soldier, but you've turned me back into a prince with your bravery." He took my hand. "And you are my princess."

How warm his hand was, and how steadily his eyes looked into mine. I was shy and dizzy with happiness. Was this how it felt to be in love? I looked down, and my nightdress had become a shimmering ball gown, and there were jewels at my throat and in my hair.

"Come with me," he said.

The walls of our house seemed to float away from us then, and we were outside in the night. A swarm of snowflakes flurried round us and lifted us up as if we were no weight at all, carrying us away from the darkened houses and the spires and buildings of my town. I was not afraid; I was with my prince. The snowflakes melted, the stars fell away from the sky and the sun rose like a golden ball. We were in a boat with blue wings, and we sailed towards an island palace that was made of sugared ice.

"Where are we?" I asked, but I knew in my heart that this was the kingdom of sweets, and that the floating palace that we were being drawn towards was glittering with candy, twists of barley sugar, lemon drops, honeyed whirls and peppermint. A princess in a deep red gown the colour of plums came to welcome us, smiling at me as if she had always known me.

"You've come at last," she said. "We're very honoured. Sit and feast and watch the entertainment we've prepared for you."

I have never seen such wild, funny, extraordinary dancing. People from the scented lands of tea and coffee and chocolate and spices whirled round us in their bright costumes, red taffeta and green embroidered silk, golden flowing robes; they leapt and swirled, two and two and two and two. The beautiful sugar-plum fairy and her prince flew like graceful birds, so together and so wrapped in each other that they seemed at times to be one person.

As I watched them I was filled with a strange, sad longing; I did not understand it. I was a princess too, I had my beautiful gown and my glittering jewels, I had my handsome prince and I danced in his arms. Was this the happiness of being grown up? And if it was, then why did I feel such sadness? Round and round we span, round and round. The dancers all clustered round me stroking me with their soft wings, humming quietly, and I realized that they were not people but bees, swarming like snowflakes into their sugary hive. And my prince, my nutcracker prince, let go of my hands and went with them.

I opened my eyes in a cold dark room, and for a moment I didn't know where I was. I gazed around, and the fire's last glow threw up strange shadows that slipped away to nothing. Franz's soldiers and my dolls in their coloured costumes lay scattered over the carpet, sweets spiralled on the Christmas tree, green and gold, red and blue, and at the very top the sugar-plum fairy stood poised and still and smiling. Light snow buffed the windows under a frosty moon.

And clutched in my hands was the little painted nutcracker that Godfather Drosselmeyer gave to me a long time ago, when I was a little girl, when magic really happened.